DISNEY's

Winnie the Pooh's
BEDTIME
Stories

BY Bruce Talkington   ILLUSTRATED BY John Kurtz

Disney
PRESS

NEW YORK

Contents

In Search of Breakfast

It was the very best time of day in the Hundred-Acre Wood, which is the same as saying it was the very beginning of the day, when the sun was just easing itself up over the horizon. It was the time when a certain bear of very little brain typically rolled out of bed to celebrate the new morning with a very large breakfast.

But this wasn't to be a typical morning at Winnie the Pooh's house. Instead of the friendly rattle of honeypots and hungry smacking noises, the only sound to be heard was a long, shivering sigh, followed immediately by a most forlorn "Oh bother."

Pooh was sitting on the edge of his bed, swinging his feet aimlessly and looking terribly sad. He looked as if not even the thought of breakfast would cheer him up. In fact, when the thought of his favorite time of day for a small smackeral of something sweet to eat did occur to him, he wrinkled up his forehead even more and swung his feet around a bit more nervously and said, *very* loudly, "Oh

BOTHER bother!" Some serious thinking had to be done about breakfast, and Pooh knew there wasn't enough room inside for it to take place properly. So he hopped off the bed and began to dress as quickly as he could.

In no time at all Pooh was stomping through the Hundred-Acre Wood in no particular direction as fast as his short legs could carry him.

Realizing finally that thinking was done much more constructively when seated comfortably than at a full run and all out of breath, Pooh plopped himself down on a convenient stump and tried to look as serious as it was possible for him to look for as long as it was possible for him to do so. He managed this for up to several seconds at a time, hoping that the more he looked as if he were having an idea the more likely it would be that one might come along and take root. But instead of an idea, Tigger happened along. He reacted with dismay at the uncharacteristic look of concentration on Pooh's face.

"Pooh boy," Tigger cried with great concern in his voice, "what's the matter? Thorn in your paw? Ache in your tooth? Cramp in your cramper?"

Pooh tried desperately to hang on to his serious expression as he answered, "No, Tigger, it's nothing like that. Why do you ask?"

"I'm askin' 'cause you look like you just lost your best friend," Tigger said. "An' I know that's impossibibble 'cause I was standing right next to you the last time I looked."

Pooh smiled. "You were still standing there the last time I looked, too," he said. Then he sighed as he realized that all his efforts at thoughtfulness had disappeared along with his frown.

"Then what are we waiting for?" shouted Tigger with delight. "It's time for breakfast! Let's go do what Pooh Bears and Tiggers do best and snarf down a few smackerals."

"I can't," said Pooh so very quietly that Tigger almost didn't hear him.

"Winnie the Pooh can't have breakfast?" Tigger responded in amazement. "Why not?"

"Because breakfast is what is eaten after a night's

sleep," Pooh explained sadly. "And I haven't had the sleep yet."

"I think you'd better tell me what's going on, Pooh," said Tigger solemnly.

"Well," Pooh began, thinking back, "it was a soft and cozy night, my bed was quite comfortable, and I'd just had my midnight smackeral, so there was no rumbly in my tumbly to keep me awake."

"So, what happened?" Tigger wanted to know. "Did some sort of noisy-type noise keep you awake? Creakin' faucets or drippin' floors?"

"No," replied Pooh thoughtfully, "it was the quiet I listened to all night long. There seemed to be so very much of it."

"Wow!" said Tigger. "I don't think I'd have even heard my bedtime story if all that quiet was hangin' around *me*."

"Bedtime story?" said Pooh, suddenly sitting up very straight. "*I* didn't hear any bedtime story."

"Hoo-hoo-*hoo*!" exclaimed Tigger triumphantly. "No wonder you stayed awake. How can anyone go to sleep without a bedtime story?"

"You're right, Tigger," said Pooh, laughing with relief. Then, all at once, the smile faded from his face. "Does that mean I have to wait until bedtime tonight for a story before I can fall asleep and have today's breakfast . . . tomorrow?" Pooh didn't want to think about being behind a breakfast every morning from that day on. Then he realized that if he couldn't have today's breakfast until tomorrow, today's lunch and dinner would have to be put off as well! The thought was almost more than his hungry tummy could stand.

"Naw," Tigger assured him. "A bedtime story's good anytime you go to bed."

"So that must mean breakfast is good anytime you wake up." Pooh nodded understandingly. "Now all I have to do is find one so I can have the other."

Tigger threw his arm affectionately around Pooh's shoulders. "Relax, Pooh boy," he told him. "I got a doozy of a story for you."

Once upon a Bounce

It was a typical Tuesday morning for Tigger. He bounced out of bed, bounced through his bath (splashing water everywhere in the process), bounced out his front door, and hurled himself across the Hundred-Acre Wood in a series of leaps and bounds that carried him easily over even the tallest trees until he arrived at the home of Winnie the Pooh.

As soon as Pooh opened his front door, before he could say so much as "Good morning, Tigger!" or "My, aren't you looking particularly well today!" Tigger threw his arms around the portly bear, and they rolled head over heels across the floor into Pooh's parlor.

"Hiya, buddy bear!" shouted Tigger happily as he pinched Pooh's round cheeks enthusiastically. "Are you as happy to see me as I am to be seen?"

"Hello, Tigger," Pooh answered. "I'm always glad to see you." He rubbed his face tenderly. "I'm even glad to feel you . . . most of the time."

"So, what's for breakfast?" Tigger bounced into a chair, rattling the honeypots spread out on Pooh's dining table. "It's Tuesday, you know!"

"Is it really?" responded Pooh politely. "And what exactly has Tuesday to do with you and me and breakfast?"

"Why, Tuesday's the day after Ones-day!" said Tigger with surprise. "It's the day I always come for breakfast." He tied a napkin elegantly around his neck. "One can't, after all, eat breakfast all by oneself when it's . . ."—Tigger pointed a finger at Pooh Bear—"one . . ."—then at himself—"Twos-day, can one?" He waggled his eyebrows in delight and chortled, "Hoo-hoo-*hoo!*"

Pooh was well aware that arguing about numbers only made him hungry, and he was hungry enough already. "No, one . . . I mean, two . . . can't, I suppose." He climbed onto the chair next to Tigger.

"Oh boy!" said Tigger, grabbing a pot of honey and pouring a more-than-large dollop of the sticky sweet liquid down his throat. "I love this stuff," he mumbled when he stopped eating long enough to lick his lips.

"Me, too," Pooh said quietly, watching Tigger put down the now-empty pot and snatch up a full one. Pooh had much preferred the days when Tigger had thought he didn't like honey. It had meant much larger portions for Pooh.

"You know," said Tigger after emptying his third or fourth pot of honey, "I bet you love honey as much as I love bouncin'!"

"Yes." Pooh sighed as he gazed at the growing pile of *very* empty pots. "And it always seems there's never enough of what we love the most."

Tigger stopped right in the middle of a particularly messy slurp, unaware of the honey leaking down over his nose. He gazed forlornly at Pooh. "N-not enough—of what we love the *most?*"

Pooh, his face poked deep into a distressingly empty jar, replied hollowly, "It seems so. Good things sometimes seem to just . . . run out."

Climbing slowly and carefully down from the chair, Tigger stood, flat-footed and awkward, on the wooden floor. "Thanks for the breakfast, Pooh," he said, "but I think I'll skip the rest of it. I'm not very hungry all of a sudden."

Then, sliding his feet cautiously across the floor, Tigger walked . . . slowly . . . out of Pooh's house.

Pooh, his face squinched into a puzzled frown, watched him go. He then surveyed the jumble of empty pots, crocks, and jugs scattered on his table.

"Goodness!" Pooh murmured to himself. "What would I have done if he'd been hungry?"

For the next few days the primary topic of conversation around the Hundred-Acre Wood was, What in the world is the matter with Tigger?

"It takes him forever to get from one place to another," Rabbit observed.

"When he bothers to go anywhere," whistled Gopher.

"He seems so sad," said Piglet. "He just sits around and mopes."

"And, if you don't mind my saying so," Eeyore added, "Tigger's no slouch when it comes to mopin'."

"So," demanded Rabbit, "what are you going to do about him, Pooh?"

Pooh scratched his head and considered for as long as

he thought was polite. Then he said, "I give up. What?"

"No one makes a friend feel better than you do, Pooh," said Piglet, taking Pooh's hand in his own.

"That's right," agreed Eeyore. "Just find Tigger and do what you always do."

"Oh, well," said Pooh. "I suppose I could do that."

"Of course you can, Pooh," said Rabbit, patting him on the back. "That's why we're sending you."

As Pooh wandered through the Hundred-Acre Wood looking for Tigger, he was thinking furiously, hoping he could remember what it was he always did.

So deep in thought was Winnie the Pooh that he almost stumbled over Tigger, who was sprawled on the riverbank staring gloomily at his reflection in the water, totally unaware of what was going on around him. Pooh was so surprised to see him that he didn't have to think about doing what he always did; he simply did it, blurting out a delighted-to-see-you "Hello, Tigger!"

"Yeow!" shouted the startled Tigger, bouncing several feet into the air. Landing on his feet, Tigger threw his arms around Pooh and rested his head on Pooh's shoulder. "Please, Pooh boy," he gasped breathlessly, "don't ever do that again."

"Certainly, Tigger," agreed Pooh. "But could you please tell me exactly what it is you don't want me to do?" He pulled thoughtfully on his ear. "I hope it's not what I always do . . . whatever that is."

"Just don't make me bounce like that," said Tigger. "I haven't got that many left to waste, you know."

"You haven't?" asked Pooh, very much surprised at this news. "How many bounces did you have to begin with?"

"Well," said Tigger thoughtfully, "I always figured it was one of those great big numbers that come somewhere after two." He leaned close to Pooh and continued in a whisper. "But somebody told me once, I disremember who exactackily, that good things just seem to run out sometimes."

Pooh rubbed his ear thoughtfully. "I heard someone say

that once, too," he mused. "But I can't remember who it was either, so it must not be very important."

Pooh crinkled his brow, because brows were always crinkled when thinking was taking place, and Pooh was almost positive that thinking—or something very much like it—was what he was doing at the moment.

"Besides, how can you run out of something," Pooh asked slowly, "when you don't run? You *bounce*!"

"Say," responded Tigger admiringly, "that's a pretty good question!"

"Yes, I knew it must be," said Pooh proudly, "because I certainly don't know the answer to it."

"What else don't you know, Pooh?" asked Tigger hopefully.

Pooh was now much too excited to remember to crinkle his brow. "If *up* means more, which I'm certain it sometimes does . . . ," he began.

"Sure it does," agreed Tigger, "like stocking *up* on honey, or dressing *up*, or growing *up*!"

"Then," Pooh continued, "I don't know why bounces—which all go *up*—should ever end . . . should they?"

"No sirree!" hooted Tigger joyously, launching himself upward in one tremendous bounce.

It was the most amazing bounce ever seen in the Hundred-Acre Wood.

Pooh had to sit down quickly and lean back until he was flat on the ground to keep his friend in sight.

The tallest trees in the forest suddenly felt like tiny saplings again as Tigger sailed up past them, and birds were forced to fly on their backs in order to watch Tigger grow smaller and smaller as he went higher and higher and HIGHER.

Clouds were so surprised by Tigger's passage that they thought for a moment they were upside down and Tigger was falling because no one had ever bounced that high before!

All in all, it was long past suppertime when Tigger finally returned to earth, but Pooh, hungry as he was, knew that waiting for his friend was the polite thing to do.

"Yippee!" cried Tigger, shaking Pooh's hand so vigorously that Pooh was forced to bounce in excited little circles along with him. "You did it again!"

"What, exactly, was it that I did?" Pooh wanted to know.

"Why, what you always do, Pooh boy," answered Tigger. "What you always do."

"Ah," said Pooh, still not having the slightest idea what it all meant but taking comfort in how familiar it sounded. "Well, you're very welcome."

"I'll see you tomorrow for breakfast. It's Tuesday, you know," called Tigger, who was hopscotching across the Hundred-Acre Wood, bouncing so high that a flock of geese flying south for the winter started to follow him home.

The smile faded from Pooh's face. "Breakfast?" he muttered, thinking of his cupboard full of honey. "Tomorrow?" Pooh sighed and grinned a lopsided grin. "Oh bother!"

"Are you sleeping, Pooh?" asked Tigger as he looked deep into Pooh's wide-open eyes.

"Why, no, Tigger," Pooh answered. "Are you?"

"No. This is what happens when Tiggers do what Tiggers do best." He sighed. "We're just too fascinatin' to be sleepifyin'."

Tigger leaned closer to Pooh. "Tell me, Pooh. What do you think when somebody mentions . . . vegebibbles?"

Before Pooh could answer, a large yawn overcame him.

"That's all I wanted to know," said Tigger, grabbing Pooh's arm and pulling him quickly along through the forest.

"Where are we going, Tigger?" gasped Pooh.

"To find a bedtime story that does the job it's supposed to do," replied Tigger.

The next thing Pooh knew, he and Tigger were in Rabbit's kitchen, sitting across the table from Rabbit himself.

"Bedtime story?" Rabbit was saying in surprise. "All I know about bedtime stories is that I love to listen to them, but I'm not very good at telling them." Rabbit looked embarrassed. "I hardly ever get to the end, you see."

"Why not?" asked Pooh.

"I always put myself to sleep," Rabbit admitted.

"That's just the kind we want to hear!" exclaimed Tigger and Pooh at the same time.

"Very well." Rabbit shrugged. "If you insist."

Rabbit's Rules of Order

Rabbit was acting even more like Rabbit than usual. As far as he was concerned, absolutely nothing was going right in the entire Hundred-Acre Wood. It was harvesttime in his garden and he'd suggested—suggested, mind you, he hadn't demanded anything—that it might be nice if he had a little help picking and bringing in all his fruits and vegetables. And no one had shown up! It was already five o'clock in the morning, the sun had been up for almost ten minutes, and there had not been so much as one knock on his front door from a friend ready for work!

Rabbit didn't think he was being unreasonable. He knew it wasn't his friends' garden. But what could they have to do that was more important or more satisfying than working in his fields?

"Pooh most certainly isn't even out of bed yet," Rabbit sniffed with a superior air. "Or if he is, he's eating a breakfast that will continue until lunchtime!"

Rabbit flopped down in his armchair in frustration. "And is Pooh's friend Piglet helping him along so they can get to my house for a bit of work?" he asked himself. "Of course not. Piglet's in the middle of cleaning his house again, as if it could get any cleaner!" Rabbit pulled his ears down under his chin. "And Gopher's too interested in the underground to lower himself and come up to see what happens on top of it for a change."

As he continued thinking about his friends and neighbors, Rabbit grew increasingly upset, almost tying his ears into a knot under his chin. "That annoying jester, Tigger, would rather bounce over fruit trees than help me harvest them," he complained. "And Eeyore's probably sitting in that silly old shed he calls home—if he isn't rebuilding it because it's fallen down again—thinking I meant someone else when I asked him." Rabbit sighed and leaned back in his chair.

"Anyway, even if they all did show up on time, ready to pitch in and work, they'd all go about it *inefficiently*, each of them doing chores in his own little way instead of the right way—MY way!"

Rabbit rested his very tired head in his hands. It was hard work thinking about how other people should run their lives in some sort of organized manner.

Because it was harvesttime, Rabbit had not slept at all well the night before. Now, not even aware that he had closed his eyes, Rabbit fell sound asleep, snoring gently with an occasional twitch of one ear or the other.

He dreamed a very Rabbit sort of dream. He no longer lived in the Hundred-Acre Wood. It was, instead, the Hundred-Acre Garden, and fields of ripe vegetables and overflowing fruit trees reached as far as the eye could see from Rabbit's front porch.

Rabbit rubbed his hands together in gleeful anticipation. What a wonderful harvest this would be! Then his ears began to droop as he realized it would take him so long that he'd have to start the spring planting before he'd finished harvesting.

"So, what are you waiting for?" demanded a familiar voice. Rabbit turned, and there stood Pooh, but not exactly Pooh. The silly old bear had ears just like Rabbit's clothespinned to his own and a soft, round cotton tail fastened to the back of his red jersey.

"It's time to get to work," said Pooh, thrusting a shovel into the startled Rabbit's hands and stomping off toward the fields.

"Pooh?" Rabbit breathed after him in an awestruck voice.

"Don't be silly, Rabbit," squeaked a high voice. "I'm Piglet."

Rabbit spun around and looked down in surprise to discover Piglet standing beside him next to a wheelbarrow full of freshly harvested potatoes. To Rabbit's amazement, Piglet was also sporting a pair of very small Rabbit ears and a tiny tail.

Piglet pulled a small pail and a very large scrub brush from the wheelbarrow and pushed them into Rabbit's hands, almost causing him to drop the shovel.

"These potatoes are filthy," declared Piglet. "I'm not harvesting another one until you get them cleaned up!"

Before Rabbit could utter a "But Piglet!" Tigger bounced into view, complete with Rabbit ears and tail, and dropped a basket full of apples on Rabbit's toes.

"Need to make a lot more o' these baskets if you expect to keep up with my apple pickin', bunny boy," Tigger declared. "Hop to it! It's the only way to get anything done. Hop-hop-*hop*!" Tigger leaned closer and whispered into Rabbit's ear, "I shouldn't have to be telling that to a rabbit, bunny boy." He winked and bounced off.

While Rabbit was still trying to think up an answer, Gopher, his Rabbit ears and tail dirty from digging, popped up out of the ground at Rabbit's feet and pulled a huge watering can up after him.

"No time for baskets, Rabbit," he whistled. "We have to water your crops."

"Of course we do," agreed Rabbit. "I water them all the time!"

"But you do it in such a sloppy way!" Gopher snapped.

"There's only one efficient way to water crops." He pointed down the hole. "From the roots up!"

Gopher grabbed Rabbit's elbow and pulled him toward the tunnel.

"Not so fast," brayed Eeyore as he joined the group, wearing his bunny ears and tail. "I want to know why we have to carry these fruits and vegetables to sheds to store them. Why can't we just build sheds over them?"

Pooh stomped back to the group. "Come on, Rabbit," he ordered. "We're wasting daylight. I'm afraid we're going to have to skip lunch if we're ever going to finish on time."

"But Pooh," protested Rabbit, "we haven't even had breakfast yet!"

"Don't worry, Rabbit," said Pooh as he patted Rabbit on the back. "We'll have breakfast tomorrow."

"Tomorrow?" shouted Rabbit, aghast.

"After we work all night," agreed Pooh. "Good idea, Rabbit."

"But, but . . . ," Rabbit sputtered, but it was no use. Everyone began talking at once at the top of their voices, wriggling their long Rabbity ears and shaking their round Rabbity tails. Rabbit didn't know where to look or whom to listen to, so he closed his eyes and yelled, "Help!" as loudly as he could.

Rabbit instantly woke up and heard knocking at his front door. "Thank goodness," he said with a sigh. "It was only a dream." Then he jumped out of his chair to see who was calling.

He found Pooh, Piglet, Tigger, Eeyore, and Gopher standing on his front porch, ready to help him with his harvest. Rabbit was relieved to note that the only Rabbity ears and tail to be seen were his own.

"Here we are, Rabbit," announced Pooh, "ready to work."

"Just tell us what you want us to do, long ears," said Tigger, "and we'll get it done."

"No, no!" Rabbit held up his hands in protest. "You all work the way you want to. I'm grateful for the help, but I certainly don't want to tell you how to be yourselves." He laughed nervously. "I'm sure you're all quite capable of doing what you think is best and that that's the most efficient way to go about it. And when we're done, I'll prepare you all a wonderful supper."

"My," whispered a surprised Pooh to the others when Rabbit went to fetch them some tools. "That doesn't sound like Rabbit at all."

"Oh, it's him all right," snickered Tigger. "No one else'd wear those ears and that tail!"

Pooh looked at Rabbit and Tigger. They were both fast asleep with their heads resting on the kitchen table, snoring quietly back and forth. "Well," said the very unsleepy Pooh to himself, "at least he finished the story this time."

Pooh left Rabbit's house, closing the door softly behind him, and began to stroll through the woods once again.

"Where am I going to find a bedtime story that will put me to sleep?" he asked no one in particular. "Perhaps a very small story—one that's not so large it keeps a bear awake."

He stopped his musings and smiled. "Of course! Why didn't I think of it before?"

"But Pooh," protested Piglet a few minutes later, "the only story I know by heart is one you made up about me."

"I did?" said Pooh in surprise.

"Yes, it's a poem you made up one day when I was feeling very, *very* small." Piglet shyly poked at the ground with the big toe on his very small foot. "It was about me . . . sort of."

"That sounds like a small enough story to me," said Pooh. "How does it go?"

"But Pooh, it was your very own poem," said Piglet.

"I knew what it was once," explained Pooh, "but all I remember now is that I don't remember it."

"All right, Pooh," gulped Piglet nervously. "Here goes."

A Knight to Remember

In a land of long ago
With castles high and villains low
Where happy endings always seemed the rule
There dwelt a Piglet so polite
That though he longed to be a knight
He feared to say so and appear a fool.

In his house the doors were tiny
And the floors were waxed and shiny—
Piglet never ventured far from home.
Yet while he soaped and scrubbed and cleaned
Piglet dreamed his knightly dream:
A brave and dashing Piglet on the roam!

Bright and early one spring morning
Castle bells tolled out a warning:
"A dragon's strolling through the countryside!"
All the people in the town
Quickly pulled their shutters down
And Piglet jumped beneath his bed to hide.

Then he heard his doorbell ring:
It was a message from the king!
"Alas, sweet Princess Kanga has been snatched."
Before our Piglet found the wit
To ask what *he'd* to do with it
Off to the king he found himself dispatched.

The king, who looked a lot like Pooh,
Told Piglet what he had to do
And Piglet, too polite to disagree,
Soon left the castle, scared and shaking—
Dragon's breath could easily bake him!—
But knowing that the rescue had to be.

Piglet found the dragon's cave
(He really was so very brave)
And crept inside as silent as a mouse.
Then he overheard the dragon
Doing some outrageous braggin',
Showing Kanga grandly 'round his house.

In the kitchen they stopped to rest
And discussed which would be best—
Whether honey, jam, or syrup for a topping.
Our dear Piglet grew quite bold;
The dragon he began to scold,
"This talk of Kanga for breakfast will be stopping!"

But the dragon gave a cry:
"Eat her? No, I'd rather die!
I'd never harm Her Highness, she's too nice.
Since my pancakes always char
And she's the greatest cook by far,
I asked her home to give me some advice."

Later all were quite delighted
When a giant stove was lighted
And pancakes were prepared for all around.
Pooh, the king, was very funny
His topping was a heap of honey
Without a single pancake to be found.

The princess had been very flattered—
Piglet had thought she really mattered!
He hadn't known the dragon was quite sweet.
So Kanga took him into service—
Guarding her he's never nervous.
A princess for a friend is really neat!

So Piglet's now a knight in armor.
Kanga thinks he's quite a charmer
And that his bright steel suit is very snappy.
The dragon cooks for Pooh, the king
(That bear will eat most anything),
And so our ending's very, very happy!

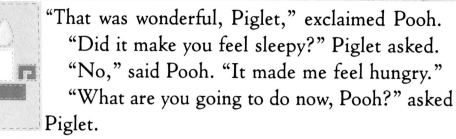

"That was wonderful, Piglet," exclaimed Pooh.

"Did it make you feel sleepy?" Piglet asked.

"No," said Pooh. "It made me feel hungry."

"What are you going to do now, Pooh?" asked Piglet.

"Ask the advice of someone who knows so very much he's forgotten almost all of it," decided Pooh.

"You're going to tell me a story?" hooted Owl with delight. "Why, that's wonderful, Pooh. Go right ahead. I love stories."

"No, Owl, you don't understand," said Pooh. "I need *you* to tell *me* a story."

"Even better!" exclaimed Owl. "Just sit down and stop interrupting."

Owl's Well That Ends Well

It was the time of year that the inhabitants of the Hundred-Acre Wood called fall because that was when the leaves on the trees decided to do just that. Transforming from green to all those bright autumn tints and hues was obviously quite exhausting. So, before the cold of winter arrived to redden the ends of noses and tickle toes (no matter how warmly cradled in sensible boots, and stockings so woolly that a pastureful of them would make a shepherd look twice), the leaves would drift drowsily down to sleep away the season under the blankets of snow that would soon be arriving.

Making sure the leaves were arranged properly for their long winter's nap was a responsibility Winnie the Pooh and his neighbors took very seriously, or as seriously as a bear of very little brain could take anything that didn't involve eating.

Owl was most helpful on these occasions because his

bird's-eye view enabled the others to rake the leaves neatly into convenient piles in out-of-the-way spots throughout the forest, places where they wouldn't be tripped over by unwary travelers but where they were easily available to anyone who felt like a good jump into a pile of leaves.

As the friends gathered, rakes at the ready, beneath the last tree in the Wood where one last leaf clung uncertainly to an uppermost branch, Owl flew up to encourage the straggler to let go and convince him that all would be well.

"Owl is certainly a wonderful bird to have around," said Piglet, thinking how nice it was that such care was being taken with such a very small leaf.

"Yes," agreed Rabbit. "It makes you wonder how he manages to put up with all the loneliness."

"Is Owl lonely?" Pooh wanted to know.

"Wouldn't you be if all the other birds in the Wood were flying south for the winter except you?" answered Rabbit.

"Well, there are no other Tiggers in the Wood and *I'm* not lonely," Tigger pointed out.

"In case you haven't noticed," Eeyore rumbled, "you're not a bird."

"Oh yeah," said Tigger. "I forgot."

"And no wonder," whistled Gopher. "With all that bouncing you do, you spend more time with your head in the clouds than Owl does."

"Than Owl does what?" Owl asked as he drifted to earth next to the last floating leaf, which Piglet recovered and tenderly put in its proper place. "Am I not doing something?"

"You're not flying south for the winter," Rabbit informed him.

"Of course not," huffed Owl, puffing out his chest in what he hoped was a very dignified manner. "I never go anywhere without an invitation."

"But you're a *bird*," Tigger reminded him, "and I'm not!"

Owl gave Tigger a very long look down his beak. "I am very well aware," Owl replied at last, "of at least one of those facts. Probably both."

"What Tigger is trying to say," said Rabbit, "is that you *have* been invited."

"Indeed?" exclaimed Owl, his already wide-open eyes opening even wider in surprise. "By whom?"

"No, not by *whom*," corrected Pooh. "By Mother Nature."

"I don't believe I know the lady," Owl answered thoughtfully.

"She's the one who says if you're early enough you catch the worm," Gopher reminded him.

"Yes," said Owl. "That's very true, but I could never see much use in spending a great deal of time in the company of worms, especially first thing in the morning."

"She also says that we should give you a hand," Eeyore

interjected, "because you're worth two birds in the bush."

At that all Owl's neighbors broke into a spontaneous round of enthusiastic applause. Owl acknowledged the ovation with quick, embarrassed bows of his head.

"Obviously," Owl said when the clapping was over, "this is a lady of quality who knows what she's talking about. South for the winter it is."

In no time at all, Owl had shaken hands with all his friends and bidden them a fond farewell. Then, after finding the most suitable limb for a dignified, but dramatic, takeoff, he spread his wings and launched himself majestically into the sky.

Pooh and the others waved and cheered and shouted good-byes until Owl disappeared from sight.

"Well," Rabbit said with a sigh, "now he won't be lonely anymore."

"Yes," said Pooh slowly, "but what about us?"

"What about us?" Rabbit repeated, confused.

"Aren't we going to be lonely without Owl?" clarified Piglet.

"Shucks," sniffed Tigger, "I miss the old feather duster already."

"Me, too," said Gopher. "That wise old bird and I had a lot in common."

"Like what?" demanded Rabbit.

"Trees, that's what!" Gopher snapped back. "Sure, he liked the tops while I found the roots positively fascinating, but a tree's a tree and nothing else!" Gopher shook his finger in Rabbit's face for added emphasis.

"I miss him, too," grumbled Eeyore, "in case anyone's interested."

Pooh leaned close to Rabbit and spoke quietly into his ear. "You miss him too, don't you, Rabbit?"

"Of course I do," answered Rabbit sadly, "but this is for his own good . . . isn't it?"

Pooh looked very thoughtful. He knew this for a fact because he could feel that his face was all scrunched up and crinkly.

"Doesn't Mrs. Nature," he said at last, "mention something about birds wearing the same suits?"

"Birds of a feather flock together," quoted Rabbit. "What about it?"

"Perhaps *we* miss flocking with Owl," suggested Piglet.

"But we don't have feathers!" Rabbit pointed out.

"Not on the outside," said Pooh, "but I think we do on the inside. That's what tickles us so when we're all together."

Rabbit looked around at all his sad-faced friends. "What are we going to do about it, Pooh?" he asked, a twinge of desperation in his voice.

Pooh quietly took Rabbit's paw into his own.

"Don't worry, Rabbit," he said with a smile. "Mrs. Nature knows all about feathers and flocking and being together." Pooh scratched his head. "All we have to do is figure out exactly what she means."

Meanwhile, somewhere deep in the Hundred-Acre Wood, Owl was perched thoughtfully on a stump.

"South," he repeated to himself for the hundredth time. "The sun sets in the west and rises in the east."

Owl looked up at the sun. It was noon, so the yellow orb was hanging right in the middle of the sky.

"That's no help," muttered Owl. He thought some more, shifting his weight from one foot to the other.

"Moss grows on the north side of a tree," quoted Owl. He looked around and sighed. "Now if I only knew which tree they were referring to."

He sat and thought some more. All at once his eyes opened wide with delight, and he breathed a sigh of relief.

"If I'm supposed to be flying south," he reasoned, "Mother Nature will obviously let me know if I'm going in the wrong direction!"

Reassured, he lifted off into the sky once more. Soaring over the Hundred-Acre Wood, Owl reveled in the view of his home. He was beginning to feel very sad at leaving it when suddenly, in a clearing far below, he saw a very strange sight.

"This bears investigating," he said to himself, swooping down for a closer look.

Landing in the clearing, Owl discovered a group of birds of various sizes, all wearing what looked to be feathers bearing a marked resemblance to his own. They all were also wearing very pinched expressions on their faces.

"Excuse me," said Owl as politely as he could, "but are you in pain?"

"No," said one of the birds with a chuckle that sounded very much like Pooh's, "we're just looking *wise*."

"Is this south?" Owl wanted to know. "If it is, it looks very much like home."

"It is home, Owl," said a particularly long-eared bird. "Welcome back."

"Is that you, Rabbit? And Pooh! Tigger! Why are you all dressed up in feathers?" Owl asked in amazement.

"Well, Pooh was sure Mother Nature knew where you belonged," explained Piglet, "and she mentioned feathers and flocking and so . . . here we are!"

"Well, it's most thoughtful of you all, I'm sure," Owl told them. "I'm very glad to be back. I must admit to missing you all very much."

"We missed you, too, Owl," cried Tigger, bouncing in an excited circle and sending his not-very-well-attached feathers flying everywhere.

"As far as we're concerned," Rabbit told Owl, "you never have to fly south again."

"No," agreed Owl. "If nothing else, it would be a total waste of time. Flying south is what brought me right back here!"

"Of course it did," exclaimed Pooh. "This is where Mother Nature knew you should be. And," he added with a wide smile, "everyone knows mothers always know best!"

"The trouble is, you see," said Pooh with as much exasperation as it is possible for a Pooh Bear to exasperate (which is a very small amount indeed), "that I like all these stories too much for them to put me to sleep."

"Then I know exactly who you should speak to next," hooted Owl.

"Who?" Pooh hooted back.

"I need a story that's going to put me to sleep," said Pooh.

Gopher scratched his head with the tiny pick he was using to put the finishing touches on a new tunnel. "Well," he said when the itch had disappeared, "most of the things I like to do are pretty exhausting. Could be listening to my storytelling's just as strenuous."

Pooh put on one of Gopher's extra mining helmets and sat down on a boulder with just the right amount of round-ness to make sitting satisfying. "I'm ready, Gopher."

Gopher's Day Off

It was difficult for Gopher to tell exactly what sort of day it was in the Hundred-Acre Wood. Not that he was uninterested—quite the contrary. When a gopher spends all his time underground, changes in the weather are happenings of great interest. But Gopher was a tunneler. As Tigger might say, making pathways underground was what Gophers did best. Sunshine or rain, stillness or blustery breezes would simply have to wait until Gopher had completed his latest project. And now his latest project was almost complete. He had only one more passageway to dig, and the main hallway connecting all his underground mazes would be finished!

After drawing a large **X** with his finger on the blank wall of soil before him, Gopher spit on his paws and rubbed them together in anticipation. He grasped his pick fiercely, whistled a brief tune between his teeth, and smiled happily.

"One," he counted, getting an even firmer grip on the handle of his extra-large pick. "Two," he continued, swinging the heavy pick so high over his head that the weight of it almost pulled him over backward. "Three, by dinghy!" he shouted, driving the sharp point deep into the wall of earth.

Kersploosh! A stream of water squirted through the hole made by the pick and thoroughly drenched Gopher. But more surprises were yet to come. Before he could pull the pick free, the entire wall of soil collapsed under a rush of water from the river next door, and Gopher was swept swirling down his tunnels before it.

Meanwhile, in a field some distance away, Winnie the Pooh and his friends Piglet, Tigger, Rabbit, and Eeyore were seated around a blanket spread on the soft green grass. An array of food that included everyone's favorite snacks was arranged on it.

"What I like best about picnics," said Pooh, happily smacking his lips, "is the PICNIC!"

"Me, too," agreed Tigger as he picked up a rather large sandwich. "Although the food's pretty nice, too. Hoo-hoo-*hoo*!"

"It's too bad Gopher couldn't join us," remarked Piglet as he carefully tied a napkin around his very small neck.

"He told me he had too much excavating to do," droned Eeyore sadly. "If anyone's interested in what anyone told me, that is."

"Humph!" said Rabbit. "Not even I can work all the time. He should be thinking about vacations instead of excavations, if you ask me."

"Oh," said Pooh, pulling his sticky face out of an almost empty honey jar. "I think he's too busy digging to think about either of those things."

Before anyone could explain to Pooh that digging and excavating were very much the same thing, the ground beneath the picnic emitted a low rumble.

"Excuse me," said Pooh, thinking it was his tummy saying how much it was enjoying the picnic, too.

But then the ground gave a vigorous tremble. Suddenly, at the other end of the clearing, a geyser of water spurted out of the entrance to one of Gopher's tunnels.

"My goodness," exclaimed Pooh as the water splashed over them, "it seems to be raining . . . upside down!"

The next thing anyone knew, Gopher came popping out of the tunnel atop the geyser, flew high into the air, and landed with a crash right in the middle of the picnic.

As the water ceased to spurt and Gopher tried to disentangle himself from assorted fruits, vegetables, and thistles (picked just the way Eeyore liked them), his friends were at a loss as to exactly what to say.

Finally, Pooh decided it was always beneficial to be polite when one wasn't precisely sure what was going on around one, which Pooh, for one, certainly wasn't . . . precisely. This is why, of course, Pooh was the most polite inhabitant of the Hundred-Acre Wood.

"Welcome, Gopher," Pooh began with a warm smile. "We're glad that you could come to . . . er . . ." Pooh watched for a moment as Gopher sat dejectedly in the middle of the blanket full of goodies, then continued, "I mean, *on* our picnic!"

"Well," whistled the indignant Gopher, "you can bet I'm not going to miss any more outings."

"You mean you've finished your tunnels?" asked Rabbit.

"No sir," snapped Gopher. "I mean I'm finished *with*

my tunnels! All that work and what have I got to show for it? Holes full of mud and a tail full of potato salad!"

Gopher stepped off the blanket and sat down next to his friends with a determined thump.

"But what'll you do if you're not going to tunnel?" Tigger wanted to know. "Aren't tunnels what Gophers do best?"

"I hope not," said Gopher with a sigh. "I didn't do very well with these. I think I'll just help you all for a while. Maybe we'll find something else I can do."

And Gopher was as good as his word. Pooh was the first to experience his helping paw.

It seemed there was a very large hollow tree full of a very large amount of honey collected by a swarm of very large bees. Pooh had tried and tried to climb the tree, but it was much too smooth and slippery, and the honey was located, as Pooh put it, very "up" off the ground.

Gopher happened along and discovered Pooh rocking back and forth on his heels and looking up longingly at the tree.

"Can't reach it, eh, Pooh?" asked Gopher, taking in the situation at a glance.

"I can reach it all right," said Pooh, "but only with my eyes. My arms aren't nearly long enough."

"I can fix that in no time," whistled Gopher professionally. He set to work digging furiously near the base of the tree as Pooh watched in growing wonder.

It seemed that hardly any time had passed at all before Gopher had opened up a large tunnel leading down under the hollow tree.

"How's that, Pooh Bear?" asked Gopher as he brushed the dirt off his paws.

"Well," said Pooh, looking so far down into the deep hole that his voice echoed, "it certainly seems very nice . . . but what is it exactly?"

"It's a passageway so you can get into the tree from underneath," explained Gopher proudly. "It lets you crawl inside and get to the honey."

"Yes," said Pooh as a very loud humming sound echoed back up out of the hole, "but doesn't it also let the bees get out—to us?"

"Oops!" yelled Gopher. He and Pooh turned and ran away as fast as their legs would carry them as the bees swarmed out of the excavation and, with an angry buzz, gave chase.

The next day Gopher wandered into Rabbit's garden as Rabbit was planting celery seeds for the following summer's harvest.

"Say, now," said Gopher as he watched Rabbit placing the seeds into small holes he had dug, then covering them gently with earth, "need any help?"

"Why, yes, Gopher, I do," answered Rabbit, delighted to have a volunteer. "Could you plant the rest of these seeds while I go untangle my tomato plants?"

"Absolutely," Gopher assured him as he took the spade out of Rabbit's paws. "Glad to be of assistance."

Rabbit went off to tend his tomatoes as Gopher happily dug into the rich, dark earth.

When Rabbit returned a short while later he found a very large hole in the middle of the celery patch with Gopher at the bottom of it singing to himself.

"Gopher?" Rabbit called down into the hole. "Is that you?"

"'Course it's me!" Gopher's voice drifted hollowly up

from the immense hole. "Is this deep enough for your seeds, Rabbit?"

Rabbit's ears drooped, and he gave a weary sigh. "Yes, Gopher. I believe it's quite deep enough. Thank you."

Later that same afternoon, when dark clouds were gathering in the sky above the Hundred-Acre Wood, Gopher discovered Eeyore trying to repair the roof on his home of sticks.

" 'Lo, Eeyore," Gopher greeted the donkey. "What's up?"

"Not my roof, that's for sure," Eeyore answered sadly around the stick he was holding in his mouth. "I was hoping I'd finish before it started to rain."

"Never mind the roof, Eeyore," advised Gopher. "What you need is a basement!"

"Really?" asked Eeyore, his droopy ears perking up in surprise. "Well, I'm not one to argue, so how do I go about getting one?"

"Just leave it to me," Gopher assured him, and set to work.

Before Eeyore knew it, Gopher had dug a huge basement under the little house of twigs and sticks. Unfortunately, it was so huge that after some creaking and some leaning this way and that, the house finally gave up and collapsed into the hole with a loud CRASH! Eeyore surveyed the pile of sticks scattered on the bottom of the large hole.

"Well," he rumbled, trying to look on the bright side of things, "it certainly is a nice basement for storing sticks."

"I'm sorry, Eeyore," said Gopher sadly. "I don't seem to be much good for anything lately."

Eeyore tried to think of something hopeful to tell Gopher, but the despondent rodent wandered off into the woods as the first drops of rain began to fall. Eeyore decided it was the perfect time to pay a visit to Piglet, who happened to have the best roof in the forest.

Eeyore wasn't the only one familiar with Piglet's snug roof and well-stocked larder. When the donkey arrived in the middle of the pouring rain, thundering thunder, and

lightning lightnings, he found Tigger, Rabbit, and Pooh there before him.

As the friends sat around Piglet's cozy kitchen table, the conversation turned to Gopher.

"He's just not fitting in anymore," said Rabbit.

"That's 'cause he's not doing what Gophers do best," Tigger pointed out. "He should be diggin' tunnels, not anything else."

"But how can we convince him of that?" asked Piglet. "What do you think, Pooh?"

"I think," said Pooh, who hadn't been listening to the conversation at all but instead was looking out of Piglet's window at the downpour, "that our river seems to be quite too full of itself."

The others gathered at the window to see what Pooh was referring to. They saw that the stream that usually flowed peacefully past their homes was so full of rainwater that it was on the verge of overflowing its banks.

"Oh my goodness!" screeched Rabbit in horror. "It's going to flood our houses!"

The friends ran to the front door and threw it open. Standing on the doorstep, drenched and dripping, was Gopher.

"Good," he said when he saw the surprised faces of all his friends. "Now I can apologize to you all at once."

"No time for that now, Gopher," squeaked Piglet anx-

iously. "It appears we're all about to be washed away!"

"And there's not a thing we can do about it," moaned Rabbit, looking at the surging water hopelessly.

"Oh yeah?" snapped Gopher. "Just watch this!"

Gopher hurried to a nearby tunnel entrance and quickly dropped out of his friends' view. Wading through the mud and debris still visible from the earlier flooding, he made his way to a tunnel wall that bordered on the river. He could hear the water roaring by on the other side.

Locating a discarded pick, Gopher gripped it tightly and said to himself through teeth gritted in determination, "Now to do what I do best!"

He stabbed deep into the wall with the spade, and the wall immediately gave way as river water poured in and—

once again—swept Gopher swirling away through his tunnels.

Later, when the storm had passed and the sun was peeking through what remained of the dark clouds, Gopher found himself sitting—once again—in the midst of a muddy field. He'd landed there after being ejected from one of his tunnels by a familiar geyser of water. Before he could pick himself up, however, he found himself surrounded by his friends, who immediately began slapping him on his muddy back and shaking his dirt-encrusted paws, spattering droplets of mud all over themselves and not minding it at all.

"You did it, Gopher," said Pooh excitedly. "You saved our homes from a wetting!"

"All that extra water flowed into your tunnels instead of flooding our helpless houses," exclaimed Rabbit with a tear in his eye. "Thank you, Gopher."

"You're a hero!" shouted Tigger, bouncing around the soggy clearing and covering everyone with even more mud.

"Don't be silly, Tigger," whistled Gopher modestly. "I was only tunneling. I forgot how important my work was. Never should've stopped."

"I'm sorry your tunnels were flooded again, Gopher," said Piglet in his sympathetic way.

"Thanks, Piglet, but I'll have them all in tip-top shape

in no time," said Gopher happily. "After all, tunnels are what I do best, you know."

"No, Gopher," said Pooh, putting his arm around the shoulders of his very dirty friend. "What you do best is help your friends out of trouble."

Gopher beamed up at Pooh. "I like the sound of that, Pooh Bear. I really do."

"You don't look very tired to me," said Gopher to the smiling Pooh when the story was over.

"No," agreed Pooh. "The story didn't make me tired, just happy."

"Well," said Gopher, "then I suppose you should visit someone who makes you feel droopy whether he's telling you a story or not."

"Yes," Pooh replied. "I suppose I should."

"I don't know why you'd want to hear a story from me," grumbled Eeyore.

"Please, Eeyore," pleaded Pooh. "It's very important. It has to do with breakfast and not having any."

"All right, Pooh Bear," said Eeyore somberly, "but remember—you asked for it."

Prince Eeyore

It was a very warm day in the Hundred-Acre Wood, and Eeyore had been walking for a long time. He was hot and weary and sad, mostly because his tail had fallen off sometime after breakfast, and he'd spent the hours since then walking back and forth over his footsteps searching for it without success.

He'd thought about asking his friends for help but discovered them all gathered in Rabbit's garden pushing and tugging on a large boulder located smack in the middle of the carrot patch. They were all panting and wheezing and seemed to be having such a good time (although Eeyore wasn't quite sure whether they were trying to push the boulder *into* the garden or haul it *out*) that Eeyore didn't want to trouble them with his own very personal little problem.

And now, after all that tracking without stopping for a single moment—not even for a bite of lunch—Eeyore was all but ready to give up.

"No one would even notice I was missing something except for a certain part of me that dislikes drafts and tends to get lonely," he grumbled to himself. He let out a deep sigh. "But how will I wave 'Good-bye' and 'Hello' and 'How are you this morning?' without my tail?"

Eeyore sat down in the cool shade cast by a tall elm tree.

"Nope," he decided, "I'll just have to find it myself." All at once Eeyore was trying to stifle a yawn that had crept up on him unawares, but the yawn wouldn't hear of being stifled.

"Just as soon as I have a little rest," Eeyore rumbled when the yawn was finished with him, "I'm going to find that tail for sure." The yawn returned and stretched Eeyore's mouth open even wider.

"It would be nice to have someone else doing the finding for me," he murmured, his eyelids almost too heavy to hold themselves up any longer. "It would be nice to have someone else doing everything for me," he added after a little more thought. "Not that I'll ever have the chance to find out."

Before Eeyore could say another word or think another thought, his eyes closed and he was asleep.

It seemed to Eeyore that he'd only been dozing for a very short time when the air suddenly was filled with the very large blaring of an even larger trumpet. He opened

his eyes to discover a smiling Pooh and Piglet standing before him, but it was a Pooh and Piglet the likes of which he'd never seen before.

"Good afternoon, Your Highness," said the one who looked like Pooh and even sounded like Pooh but certainly wasn't dressed like Pooh. This bear was wearing a bright green long-sleeved doublet and hose, curly-toed slippers with bells dangling from the tips, and—to top it all off—a cap with a bushy feather that danced in the breeze every time Pooh bowed, which he seemed to be doing frequently.

"We've been looking all over for you," said Piglet with a smile. He was clinging happily to a trumpet twice as tall as he was, and sporting an outfit exactly like Pooh's, only smaller.

"Excuse me, Pooh," grumbled the amazed Eeyore, "but is this a dream?"

"Probably." Pooh chuckled. "I don't suppose you'd find me dressed like this if it wasn't . . . would you?"

"But it's only a dream if you want it to be, Your Tallness," Piglet added quickly. "You are the prince, after all, and your slightest whim is our command."

"Prince?" gasped Eeyore. "I'm not a prince! In fact, if you look very closely, you'll notice I'm not a whole lot more than a donkey, a little bit scruffy, and perhaps not the best company in the world . . . but I suit me pretty well."

"Oh, we're very familiar with how scruffy you are, sire," Piglet assured him.

"And it wouldn't be quite proper for us to mention that you are bad company," said Pooh, who quickly added (after a frantic nudge from Piglet), "which you most certainly are *not*!"

"But," protested Eeyore, who was growing more and more confused, "how can I be a prince? I don't have a throne, or a crown. . . ." He paused and sighed deeply before continuing. "I don't even have a tail!"

Pooh and Piglet exchanged a look of keen surprise.

"Of course you don't have a tail," exclaimed Piglet at last. "That's how we know you're the prince."

"It is?" asked Eeyore in amazement.

"Certainly," said Pooh. "Having a tail is much too much trouble for a prince. He's much more inclined to let someone else have a tail *for* him." Pooh looked at Eeyore and scratched his head. "It would probably be someone very much like you, if you weren't the prince already—which is why, of course, you haven't got a tail. You see?"

Eeyore didn't see at all and was about to say as much when Piglet raised his trumpet and rattled the leaves on the trees with another loud blast.

"What was that for?" asked Eeyore when his ears had stopped ringing.

"We're fetching you your throne and crown," answered Piglet. "Isn't that what you said you wanted?"

Before Eeyore could answer that what he *really* said he wanted was his tail, Rabbit and Tigger (both of them dressed very much like Pooh and Piglet) marched into sight, carrying an immense chair that they quickly sat Eeyore down upon.

"Comfy, Your Donkeyness?" Tigger asked politely.

Eeyore was about to answer that it wasn't precisely the most comfortable of seats, especially to someone used to having a tail, when he was interrupted by Gopher scurrying up with a most impressive-looking crown and placing it on Eeyore's head.

"How do you like that, Your Majesty?" he whistled.

Eeyore waited a moment to see if anyone else was going to interrupt, then started to say how surprised he was that such a beautiful crown could be so heavy it made one's neck ache. He should have waited a bit longer, though, because at that moment Owl swooped down and presented Eeyore with a golden platter of thistles.

"Snack, sire?" Owl hooted warmly.

Eeyore looked unhappily at the limp thistles. "I usually like 'em picked a little fresher," he said slowly. "Crisper that way," he added.

"Oh, no, Your Majesty," Owl protested, shaking out a napkin and tying it around Eeyore's neck. "These are much tastier."

"You eat thistles?" Eeyore asked.

"Of course not," Owl replied. "I only pick them."

"Is there anything else we can get for you?" asked Pooh, bowing as low as his tummy would permit.

"Well," said Eeyore, looking around at the helpful faces and deciding to try one more time, "what I really want is my tail."

After a long silence, during which everyone shifted nervously from one foot to the other, Rabbit finally said, "But sire, you don't have a tail."

"I know I don't have it," answered Eeyore as patiently as he could. "If I had it, I wouldn't want it, would I?"

That stumped everyone for a moment.

"Don't worry," a low voice spoke up that sounded very familiar to Eeyore. "I know where your tail is."

Eeyore turned, opening his mouth to thank whoever was speaking, but what he saw was such a surprise that his mouth simply remained open without a single word tumbling out.

What Eeyore saw was . . . Eeyore! Eeyore felt as though he were looking into a mirror except that the Eeyore he

was looking at wasn't sitting awkwardly on a throne with a too-heavy crown on his head and his mouth hanging open.

"Who . . . who are you?" Eeyore (*our* Eeyore, that is) stammered in wonder.

"I'm the prince," answered Eeyore (the *other* one). "And you're sitting on my throne and wearing my crown."

"I'm sorry," said Eeyore as he climbed down from the throne and carefully placed the crown on the seat.

"No need to apologize." The prince smiled. "I was out seeing what it was like *not* to be a prince, sitting on your hilltop watching the clouds and eating your thistles." The prince made a face and stuck out his tongue. "Didn't like 'em much. Too crispy."

"I told you," said Owl to Eeyore, puffing himself up proudly.

"I suppose we all like what works for us," said Eeyore with a sigh. "Where did you say you saw my tail?"

"Up on that hard rock where you sit to watch the clouds," answered the prince. "I'm afraid it's stuck in a crack, worst luck. I tried to get it out, but it was hopeless. Must be frightfully inconvenient—having a tail, I mean."

"Not if that's what you're used to," said Eeyore.

"Right," said the prince with a laugh.

"Thanks for your help," said Eeyore gratefully.

"My pleasure." The prince bowed. "I suppose that's what dreams are for."

"So this *is* a dream," said Eeyore, nodding. And at that he immediately awakened to find himself still in the shade of the tall elm tree—and feeling much better.

Without wasting a moment, Eeyore ran up to his favorite hilltop as fast as his short legs could carry him—faster, in fact, because he was quite anxious to get there.

When he arrived at the rock, huffing and puffing from his run, he found his tail exactly where the prince had said it would be, stuck in a crack beneath the huge boulder.

"C'mon, tail," said Eeyore, grasping it in his mouth, "let's go home."

Eeyore gave the tail a pull, but it wouldn't budge. It was stuck very tightly. Not to be dissuaded, Eeyore braced his feet and pulled with all his might.

After a brief struggle, the tail sprang from the crack with a loud *Pop!* and Eeyore was suddenly sitting down holding the tail in his mouth.

Before he could recover, however, he heard a loud rumbling sound and looked up to see the huge boulder under which his tail had been trapped go tumbling down the hillside.

"Oh no," moaned Eeyore around the tail in his mouth. "It's headed right for Rabbit's garden!"

As he watched he saw his friends look up at the sound of the approaching boulder and scatter out of its path. The rolling stone smashed heavily into the boulder sitting in the carrot patch, dislodging it. Then both rocks rolled harmlessly off Rabbit's property to settle happily in

the middle of the cool stream at the bottom of the hill.

"Eeyore, did you do that?" Rabbit demanded as the donkey came running down the hill with his newly re-attached tail dangling behind him.

"Well, I had a little help," said Eeyore, giving his tail a swing, "but I suppose you could say I did do it."

Rabbit threw his arms around Eeyore's neck and hugged him with delight as Pooh and the others gathered around to congratulate him.

"I didn't think we were *ever* going to get that monstrosity out of my carrots," exclaimed Rabbit. He patted Eeyore fondly. "You're a real prince of a fellow to have around, Eeyore. Thank you."

And as the rest of his friends shouted their agreement, Eeyore blushed deeply and had a most difficult time not smiling.

"It was nothing," he told them. "And as for being a prince, there may be a resemblance if you're not looking where I'm sitting."

"It's the doing that counts, not the looking," Rabbit told him.

And now Eeyore couldn't keep a wide smile from spreading over his face.

"I think my tail would be inclined to agree with you," he told his friends happily, giving his tail an affectionate shake.

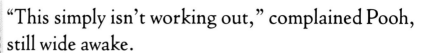

"This simply isn't working out," complained Pooh, still wide awake.

"Then there's only one thing for you to do," said Eeyore. "If you're interested, I'll tell you what it is."

"I'm very interested, Eeyore," said Pooh. "What do I have to do?"

"Find a mommy and tell her your troubles," Eeyore replied. "And we know where to find one of those."

"Yes," Pooh said happily. "We certainly do!"

"Of course I can help," said Kanga, smiling at the anxious Pooh. She sat down in her rocking chair and lifted Pooh gently up onto her lap. "You just listen and we'll get this all worked out once and for all. The most important thing for you to know is that everything is going to be all right."

"All right, Kanga," said Pooh as he snuggled down comfortably on her lap. "I'm ready."

"And remember, Pooh," Kanga reminded him tenderly one last time, "that simply *hearing* a story isn't enough. You must *listen* to it until you feel it taking place inside you."

"I'll listen, Kanga." Pooh yawned, feeling cozier than he had all day. "I promise."

Shadow Play

Dark clouds were playing tag in the night sky high above the silent Hundred-Acre Wood. As they wheeled and rushed across the face of the full moon, their shadows danced along the forest floor below and scurried through the trees in their own game of hide-and-seek.

At Kanga's house the shadows appeared to be creeping along the outside walls and peeking curiously into Roo's bedroom window.

Roo sat motionless on his bed, the covers pulled up so far that all that could be seen were his ears and wide-awake eyes. He was watching the restless shadows on the walls and ceiling as they played tricks with what little light there was.

"Mama," squeaked Roo, barely able to push the word through his throat.

At the sound of his voice, the shadows stopped moving and hovered expectantly.

"Mama," Roo repeated, a bit more loudly this time, "may I have a drink of water, please?"

"Coming, Roo, dear," answered Kanga.

As the shadows heard Kanga hopping down the hallway toward Roo's room, they instantly darted out of sight—hiding behind curtains, inside carelessly-left-open dresser drawers, and under the bed. When Kanga opened the door holding a candle and a cup of cold water, there was nothing moving but Roo, who was climbing out cautiously from beneath his cozy barricade of bedclothes.

"Is everything all right, Roo?" asked Kanga gently as she handed her son the cup of water.

"Oh, sure," replied Roo as casually as he could. "I'm just a little thirsty."

"*Very* thirsty, I would say." Kanga chuckled quietly as she watched Roo drink. "This is the third time tonight you've asked me for water."

"It's all that *yawning*," Roo answered, thinking quickly. Immediately he pretended to yawn the very biggest yawn he'd ever yawned. It stretched ever so much wider than the polite paw he raised to cover his mouth.

"See, Mother?" he said when he finally managed to get his mouth closed. "Wouldn't that make you thirsty?"

"Absolutely." Kanga smiled.

Accepting the empty cup Roo held out to her, Kanga added, almost as an afterthought, "When I was a very small girl, it was the *dark* that made me thirsty. I must have asked my mother for a glass of water a hundred times, when all I really wanted was a light. But I thought I was too old to need one anymore."

Roo grinned, and his black eyes sparkled, because he knew Kanga about as well as any child can know his mother.

"Nice try, Mama," he said, "but you said I was big enough to sleep without a night-light."

"No," Kanga reminded him, "*you* said you were big enough. I said, 'We'll see, dear.' "

"Does that mean you don't think I'm big enough?"

Roo asked, disappointment in his voice.

Kanga sat down on the bed next to Roo and put her arm around his shoulders. "Oh, no, Roo," she assured him. "That's not what I think at all."

Roo looked up at Kanga gratefully. "You don't?"

"Of course not," she said, giving him a squeeze. "I was simply wondering whether the shadows have come to visit you yet."

"Shadows?" Roo repeated cautiously. "What shadows?"

"Oh," Kanga replied. "They're very frightening, but only until you get to know them. Have you seen any?"

"Well, maybe," said Roo slowly. "What do they look like?"

"You'd know them if you saw them," Kanga said. "There's one that bounces through the window and makes the curtains flutter, especially when there's a full moon like tonight."

"And another one that likes to hide in the closet and make the clothes sway and shake like someone's in them," added Roo.

"And one that hides under the bed and rolls around until the floor creaks and moans," finished Kanga. "So you have seen them."

"Uh-huh," admitted Roo. "But what do you mean they're only frightening until you get to know them?"

"Ah," sighed Kanga, "when you find out why they're

here, it makes the nighttime so much more pleasant."

"Why *are* they here?" Roo wanted to know.

"Well," Kanga began thoughtfully, "you know when you sometimes find something in the pocket of an old jacket that you thought had been lost long ago?"

"Sure." Roo smiled. "That's always a nice surprise."

"That's the shadow in the closet," explained Kanga. "It comes across something that's been lost or forgotten and brings it back to where it will be found."

"Wow," gasped Roo.

"And the shadow that flutters the curtains wants to make sure that no one misses how beautiful the Hundred-Acre Wood looks in the moonlight," Kanga continued.

"What about the one under the bed?" whispered Roo,

not wanting to draw the shadow's attention until he was absolutely sure it was safe to do so.

"It has to do with the *floor* under the bed," Kanga whispered back. "It seems floors under beds get very little attention. No one scuffs them, or tracks mud on them, or even spills anything on them. They get very lonely as well as very dusty."

"So the shadow cheers them up," guessed Roo.

"Yes." Kanga nodded. "And it's very much like scratching a cat between the ears. Those creaks and groans are a floor's way of purring."

"That's neat!" shouted Roo, jumping up and down on his bed in excitement.

"And there are many other shadows that I don't really know anything about, but knowing the few I do to be so very friendly, I'm sure they're all just as helpful and courteous, aren't you?"

"Sure," Roo answered at the top of his voice. Then he continued more quietly. "Mama, you can go back to bed now. I don't think I'll be thirsty anymore tonight."

"All right, dear," said Kanga. She kissed Roo on the forehead. "Good night."

"Mama," said Roo as Kanga opened his door to leave.

"Yes, dear?"

"Any time you want," he said, "you can leave the light

in your room and come watch the shadows with me."

"Why, thank you, Roo," said Kanga. "I may very well do that someday." She smiled in the darkness. "Someday very soon."

"Good night, Mama."

"Good night, Roo, dear. Sleep well."

As Pooh, fast asleep on Kanga's lap, breathed gently in and out, Kanga slowly rocked back and forth in the rocking chair, filling the room with the sound of its friendly creaking. She held her finger to her lips as Tigger, Rabbit, Piglet, Owl, Gopher, Eeyore, and Roo crept quietly into the room and spread out a breakfast feast the likes of which had never been seen before in the Hundred-Acre Wood. Then they all sat down and patiently waited for their friend to awaken so they could share it with him.